MW00958476
Emmet and Olive
and the hickory tree...
Written by Katherine E. Stafford
Illustrated by Abbie M. Bruso

ISBN: 0615886337
ISBN-13: 9780615886336

Emmet and Olive

and the Hickory Tree

Written by Katherine E. Stafford

Illustrated by Abbie M. Bruso

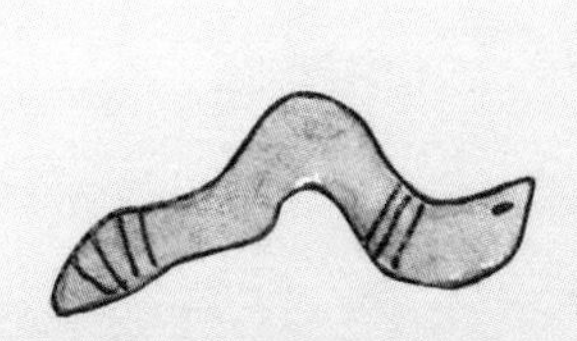

Dedicated to my very sweet,
little boy, Emmet Winchester;
my world and inspiration.

One sunny day in the mountains of May,
Emmet and Olive set out to play.
They marched through the grass and into the weeds
in search to find some hickory seeds.

"We will plant a hickory tree," said Emmet.
"It will grow to the moon and past the Red Sea.
Its branches will stretch so far and wide,
a parade of elephants can gather inside!"

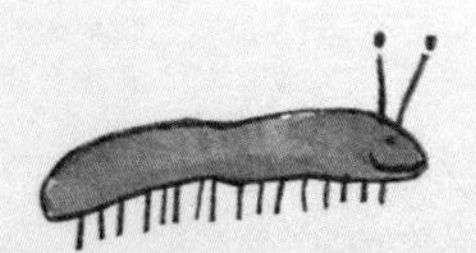

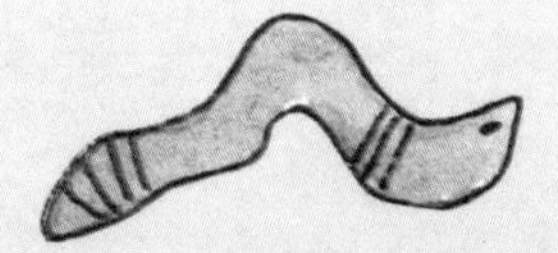

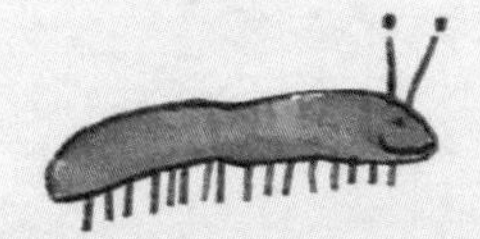

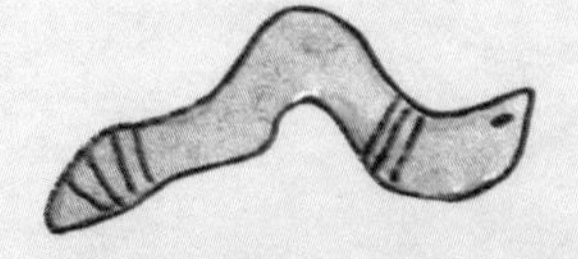

Saudi Arabia
Red Sea
Egypt

"It will grow lily pad leaves with buttercup sleeves,
and cupcakes will dangle and blow in the breeze!" Olive cheered.

"The excavator is on its way!" roared Emmet.
"We'll boom down the bucket and dig through the clay.
Get ready, Ollie, you'll need your muck boots.
We'll be diggin' up bugs, nightcrawlers, and roots!"

"I have a pink shovel," said Olive, "and I'm ready to dig,
because our tree will bear fruits both little and big.
I see sugarplum fairies and ripe apple cherries,
I can already taste the chocolate-covered strawberries!"

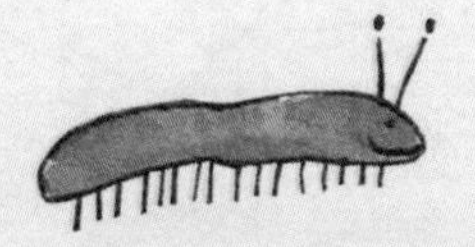

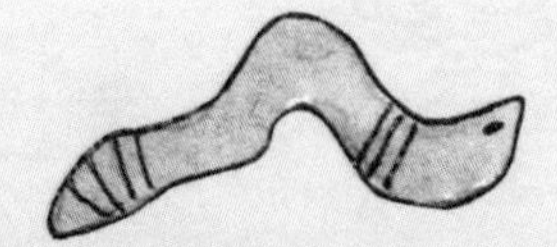

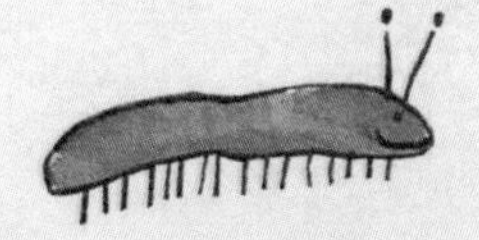

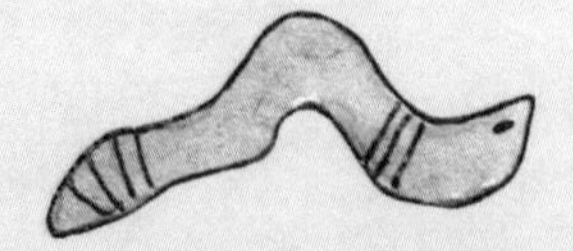

"And *I* see ice cream cones, and PB&J,
and a red robin's nest made out of soufflé!" burst Emmet.

jelly
Peanut butter

"Yes! Yes!" Olive shrieked with joy.
"And butterflies with polka-dot wings
will soar through the skies dropping pink candy rings!"

Emmet let out a hoot.
"Fishing poles will scatter our tree!
Rod, reel and sinker, they'll shine like the sea.
And fishes will swim in the pond put below,
so keep digging, Ollie, we'll need the backhoe!
We'll bring in some helpers; call Brian, where's Haley?
And Meggie will help to plant grass on our prairie!"

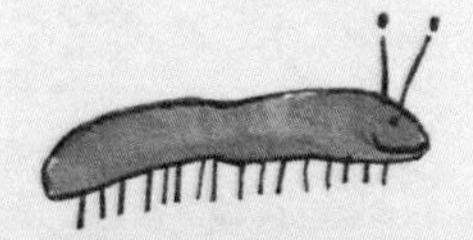
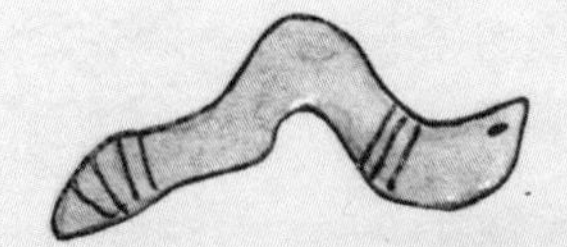
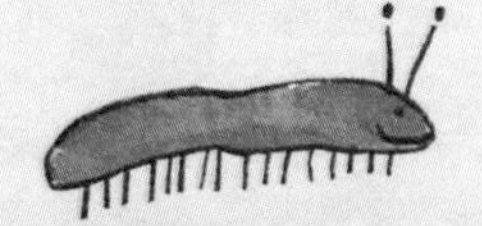
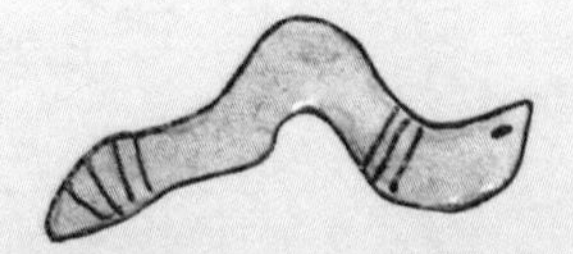

B
H
M

"Our tree will be our new favorite place.
We'll call it The Hickory Meeting Space.
Aside from all the material things,
it will also hang a big heart with wings.
There will be so much love and joy at our tree
to fill all the world, for all people to see."
Olive let out a happy sigh.

As she glanced over her shoulder, she heard not a peep,
for sweet cousin Emmet lay fast asleep.
She gave him a kiss and tucked him in tight,
and whispered ever so softly, "Goodnight."